This book belongs to

_____

Sugarplum
Mines

The
Lak

Zuckerbrote
Peak

Drosselmeyer Pl

The
Rocks

Donkey's Causeway

The Western Frostings

Dross

Th

Rocky
Falls

King
Caspar's
Mines

Rushing River

Leopard's
Paradise

The City The
Forest

s

eyer Plains

The Eastern Frosting

Valley

R. Verbena

PALEOIS/2008

Toffee-Apple
Orchards

KINGDOM OF THE FROSTY MOUNTAINS

Valentina de la Frou

Emerald Everhart

**Illustrated by
Patricia Ann Lewis-MacDougall**

EGMONT

EGMONT

We bring stories to life

Valentina de la Frou first published in 2008
by Egmont UK Limited
239 Kensington High Street
London W8 6SA

Text copyright © 2008 Angela Woolfe
Illustrations copyright © 2008 Patricia Ann Lewis-MacDougall

The moral rights of the author and illustrator have been asserted

ISBN 978 1 4052 3329 3

1 3 5 7 9 10 8 6 4 2

A CIP catalogue record for this title is available from the British Library

Printed and bound in Italy by L.E.G.O. S.P.A

Contents

Prologue 1

CHAPTER ONE: At the Grand Tea-Rooms 11

CHAPTER TWO: A Chance to Dance 31

CHAPTER THREE: Secret Post 52

CHAPTER FOUR: Rubellina Spills the Beans 68

CHAPTER FIVE: Valentina's Last Chance 80

Olympia the Eagle's Guide to Silverberg 103

Madame Malvolio's Academy Prospectus . . .113

Glossary 123

Who's Who in the Kingdom
of the Frosty Mountains 134

Prologue

When I was a young Ballerina, an admirer gave me a gift.

It was only a frosted-glass perfume bottle, filled with a sweet scent of lemon and orange. But my admirer told me that

the bottle was the most precious thing he could give, because there was a magical Kingdom inside.

I didn't believe him at first.

But that night, I had a very special dream. I dreamed of a magical Kingdom, the most beautiful land I'd ever seen, filled with delightful people and their very special animals. And the next time I danced, I thought of the Kingdom, and suddenly I danced as I had never danced before. Every night that I wore the perfume, I danced better than ever, until I was the most famous Ballerina in the world.

But one day, the old frosted-glass bottle was accidentally thrown away.

And from that day onwards, I never danced so beautifully again.

I searched for the bottle high and low, but I never found it. I have since had many years to write down what I learned about the Kingdom inside . . .

Inside the bottle, behind snow-capped Frosty Mountains, the Kingdom is divided

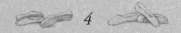

into five parts. There are frozen Lakes in the north, warmer meadows in the southern Valley, stark grey Rocks in the west, and to the east, a deep, dark Forest.

And the City. How could I forget the City? Silverberg, the capital, rising from the

Drosselmeyer Plains like a beautiful new jewel on an old ring.

From a distance, the houses seem to be piled on top of each other. Their brightly painted wooden roofs look as if they hold up the floors of the dwellings above as they wind around and around ever-more-narrow streets. And at the very top of the teetering pile is the biggest building of all: the Royal Palace. It is made from snow-white marble taken from the Frosty Mountains themselves, which glows in the

early morning sun and sparkles in the cold
night.

The Royal Palace is the home of the
King and Queen. But it is here too, within

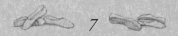

the marble walls of the Palace, that you can find the Kingdom's famous Royal Ballet School. This is where the most talented young Ballerinas in the land become proper Ballerinas-in-Training, and really learn to dance. They travel from far and wide. Pale blonde Lake girls journey from the north, dark-haired Valley Dwellers come from the south. Grey-eyed Ballerinas travel from the western Rocks, and green-eyed Forest girls make their way from the east. The City girls have no need to come quite so far.

Of course, they all bring their pets. Each Kingdom Dweller has their own animal companion. And these animals can talk – talk just like you and me. Lake Dwellers keep Arctic foxes or snow leopards, while Valley Dwellers keep small tigers, monkeys or exotic birds. Strong, sturdy Rock Dwellers enjoy the company of sheep, goats and donkeys, while Forest Dwellers keep black bears and leopards. Every City Dweller keeps an eagle.

Out there, somewhere, is my old

frosted-glass perfume bottle.

Out there, somewhere, are the Ballerinas-in-Training who inspired me — Jessica Juniper, Crystal Coldwater, Laura-Bella Bergamotta, Valentina de la Frou and Ursula of the Boughs.

And they will wait for you, until the day that you find them.

Emerald Everhart

CHAPTER ONE
At the Grand Tea-Rooms

Valentina's favourite tea-rooms in the whole of Silverberg were the smart, stylish, and terribly expensive Grand Café and Tea-Rooms. The Grand had everything. It was beautifully decorated, outside and in, with little gold chairs at marble-topped tables, and a long counter running along one side of the huge room, where you could perch up on a stool and choose your cake from a glass cabinet. And what cakes! The Grand's famous Toffee Apple Torte was sticky, shiny and utterly delicious, but if you were in the mood for something else, there were light, fruity Scoffins, hot toasted Flumpets with melted butter, or any one of another fifty-two different cakes and cookies.

Valentina, who was treated to tea at the Grand twice a year, could hardly contain her excitement when the letter arrived from her mother one bright spring morning.

'Brilliant!' she gasped, putting down her glass of Raspberry Juice with a splash. 'Mother wants to take me to tea at the Grand this afternoon! She's asked Mistress Odette for permission, and

Olympia and I are to meet her there at four o'clock.'

Olympia, Valentina's pet eagle, gave a squawk of happiness.

'Oh! Even better!' Valentina turned the letter over. 'Mother says I can bring a friend too!'

Valentina's four best friends, Jessica, Crys, Laura-Bella and Ursula, all glanced at each other.

'But Val,' said Jessica, always sensible, 'which of us will you take?'

Valentina waved a lordly hand. 'Mother won't mind if five of us turn up.'

Sinbad, Jessica's pet donkey, let out a

loud bray. 'Brilliant! I've dreamed of that Toffee Apple Torte for months!'

'I meant us five girls, Sinbad,' said Valentina. Then, seeing the donkey's ears droop, she relented. 'Well, I suppose all you pets can come too.'

Sinbad clattered his hoofs in excitement. Dorothea, Ursula's pet bear, and Pollux, Crys's white fox, looked thrilled, and even Mr Melchior, Laura-Bella's stern little tiger, gave a purr of pleasure.

'But you'll have to behave yourselves around my mother, Sinbad,' Valentina went on. 'That goes for all of you, girls and pets! Mother can be awfully snooty. I've often had to point it out to her.'

Jessica and the others kept their smiles to themselves. As much as they loved Valentina, they could not deny that she was rather snooty herself.

They dressed up in their smartest clothes straight after classes that afternoon, and hurried down the hill from the school into the streets of Silverberg. There was a hustle and bustle outside the doors of the Grand Tea-Rooms, as ladies and gentlemen came and went, dressed in all their finery.

'Do you think we're smart enough?' Sinbad hissed in Jessica's ear. 'I couldn't find my best hat – will my second-best do?'

Valentina overheard him. 'You all look perfectly smart – but Mother might disagree!'

Valentina's mother was waiting at a little table for two. It was already laid with dainty cups and plates, and a small dish of cakes was in the middle. She looked rather annoyed at having to move to a larger table, and even more annoyed when the entire plate of cakes seemed to disappear, mysteriously, shortly after Sinbad's arrival.

'How nice to meet all your friends, Val, darling,' said Mrs de la Frou. Her hair was golden, just like Valentina's, although it was wound up in a glossy coil on the back of her head, and she wore a spectacular red hat. She was plumper than Valentina, and her sweet, rather pretty face had a pouting look about it. The eagle on her shoulder was on the plump side too. It flapped a welcoming wing at Olympia, Valentina's eagle, and then stared longingly at Sinbad. 'You must be Jessica, Crystal, Laura-Bella and Ursula. I've heard so much about you! And your lovely pets

too. What a very handsome tiger and fox. And what a sweet bear! And . . . well, what a . . . donkey.'

Sinbad nodded his head, trying to hide the fact that his cheeks were bulging with cakes.

It didn't work.

'I think we shall need more cakes, waiter,' said Mrs de la Frou, with a frown, before turning to Valentina. 'Val, darling, I've got some very exciting news for you and Olympia.'

'What news?' Valentina started to pour tea for all her friends from the silver teapot, as the waiter brought more cakes. Then she gasped. 'Have you bought me that silvery necklace I wanted?'

'No, Valentina . . .' said Mrs de la Frou.

'Have you planned me a surprise birthday party?'

'No, Valentina . . .'

'Have you had my whole bedroom painted pink?'

'No, Valentina, and I wish you would let me speak!' Mrs de la Frou pushed at her hair with a fluttering hand. 'The news is much more important than that.'

'More important than a party or a pink bedroom?' Valentina frowned. 'I don't understand.'

Her four friends exchanged smiles.

'Val, darling, I am delighted to tell you that you have been accepted into Madame Malvolio's Academy for Better-Brought-Up Young Ladies!' Mrs de la Frou beamed. 'You will be starting there next term.'

The entire table fell silent, apart

from Sinbad's chomping.

'But Mother,' Valentina said, 'I already go to school. At the Royal Ballet School, remember?'

Mrs de la Frou gave a little shriek. 'Val, darling, you didn't think you were going to stay there forever, did you? You'll have a much better education at Madame Malvolio's! They teach you how to cut open a boiled egg without breaking the yolk! They teach you how to plait your hair in eighty-three styles!

They teach you how to fold a napkin into the shape of an peacock!'

Sinbad whispered to Jessica, 'I want to go to Madame Malvolio's Academy. That's all useful stuff!'

'It will be wonderful, Valentina. I only wish I had been given the chance to go to Madame Malvolio's when I was your age.' Mrs de la Frou sighed, and helped herself to a hot buttered Flumpet. 'Oh, my dear girls, you mustn't all look so horrified! You can still keep in touch with Valentina with little letters and notes. Madame Malvolio teaches the most wonderful letter-writing classes!'

'But Mother, I don't want to go to Madame Malvolio's!' Valentina burst out. 'I don't want to learn how to eat a boiled egg, or how to plait my hair, or fold napkins into silly shapes! I want to stay at the Royal Ballet School, with all my friends, and learn how to be a dancer!'

'Valentina,' said Mrs de la Frou, in a

warning tone, 'you begged me to let you
go to ballet school, and I agreed. But
your school reports have not convinced

me that you will ever be a great prima ballerina. No, no – Madame Malvolio's is the place for you. I have made up my mind. I simply won't hear another word about it.'

And so the rest of the tea, despite the wonderful treats and the gorgeous surroundings, passed by in complete, miserable silence.

CHAPTER TWO
A Chance to Dance

'How are we going to help Valentina?' asked Jessica, gathering the three others around her washbasin as she brushed her teeth before bed that evening.

'She doesn't want to leave – and we can't let her!'

'We'll have to help Val convince her mother that she's a good dancer after all,' said Laura-Bella. 'Then she'll have to let her stay.'

Their four pairs of eyes met in the mirror. This was not going to be easy. Even Valentina's top marks in Costume, Hair and Make-up could not make up for the fact that she was always at the bottom of the class for Ballet.

Just then, the bathroom door flew open and Nettie Treehouse burst in, waving her toothbrush and squirting toothpaste everywhere in her excitement.

'Have you heard?' Nettie gasped. 'A notice has just gone up in the Common Room – the Palace Theatre needs one of us Beginners to dance the part of a lonely young servant girl in their new ballet! Anyone who wants to audition has to write her name on the list in the

Common Room. I'm already the first on the list!'

And off Nettie dashed, to spread the news amongst any of the Beginners who hadn't already heard her yelling.

Jessica and her friends stared at each other.

'Are you thinking the same as me?' Jessica asked. 'If Valentina got the part, her mother would have to let her stay.'

'A part with the real, grown-up

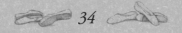

Palace Company,' Ursula breathed. 'Mrs de la Frou would let her stay for sure.'

'There's just one small problem,' said Laura-Bella, jabbing Crys in the ribs with her toothbrush. 'Crys is bound to get the part. Or maybe you, Jess – everybody knows you're the two best in the class.'

Crys and Jessica glanced at each other, blushing. 'Then we just won't audition,' Crys said.

Ursula frowned. 'Even if you don't audition, everybody else in the class will. And poor Valentina won't stand a chance.'

Crys let out a sudden yelp that startled her fox, Pollux, so much that he fell off her shoulders and into a puddle of water on the bathroom floor.

'She might have a chance – if we all help her,' Crys said.

Jessica's eyes lit up. 'What a great idea, Crys! We can help her make up a

really good audition dance, and make her practise and practise . . . we'll give up every spare minute.'

Suddenly, Valentina herself put her

golden head around the bathroom door. 'You four look as thick as thieves,' she pouted. 'Have you heard about these auditions? Aren't you coming to write your names down?'

'None of us is going to audition, Val,' said Jessica, taking Valentina by the elbow and starting to pull her towards the Common Room. 'But you are! Now, listen to our idea . . .'

Sure enough, Jessica, Crys, Laura-Bella and Ursula were the only members of the class who did not put their names on the audition list. Valentina was so grateful for her friends' plan to help that she cried and cried all through Costume, Hair and Make-up class, which Mistress Babette did not mind, and History of Ballet class, which Master Silas did.

'Blasted Palace Company,' Master Silas grumbled, 'getting you lot over-excited about their silly auditions. It's time that would be better spent doing

History of Ballet homework, if you ask me.'

But nobody else agreed with him.

That evening, Valentina and her friends gathered in an empty practice room to work out a dance routine for her audition. But although Crys worked hard to think of the simplest steps possible, Valentina struggled and struggled to get them right. Finally she just sat down on the floor and refused to get up.

'It's the nerves,' she sighed. 'They're making me worse than ever! Even Sinbad could dance these steps better than me.'

Fortunately, Sinbad took this as a compliment.

Valentina's nerves were even worse the next morning when a surprise visitor showed up at their Ballet class.

Just as Mistress Camomile was leading them all through their warm-ups, the door opened. In swept a tall, beautiful young woman, all dressed in white, with tumbling dark hair. She carried her tiny, elegant tiger in her handbag.

Everybody recognised her at once. It was Aurora Rosmarino, the Palace Ballet Company's prima ballerina.

'Miss Rosmarino!' gasped Mistress Camomile, dropping a curtsey, and waving her hands at the Beginners to do the same. 'This is an honour indeed!'

'Oh, don't mind me, Mistress Camomile.' Aurora Rosmarino took a seat, and smiled at them all. 'Please, continue with your lesson. I'll just sit here and watch, if I may.'

Her tiger yawned and snuggled down to sleep.

'She's come to see who ought to get the part!' hissed Sinbad, who as usual was clip-clopping about at the back of the class, trying to keep time to the music.

Jessica knew that Sinbad was right. She caught Crys's eye, and her friend nodded. Crys knew just what Jessica meant. They must both be sure to dance

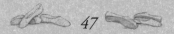

very badly in class today, so that Aurora Rosmarino would not notice them and tell them to audition.

As the class went on, Jessica and Crys did everything they could to dance badly. They bumped into each other, and the walls, whenever possible, and deliberately messed up even the easiest steps. When Jessica fell over during her pirouettes, Mistress Camomile had seen enough, and sent her to sit at the back until the lesson was over.

'Getting nervous, are you?' Rubellina Goodfellow taunted Jessica as they all left the practice room. 'Some girls just aren't cut out to dance in front of important people.'

Jessica ignored her.

'No wonder you and your friends didn't put your names down to audition,' Rubellina continued, giggling. 'Too scared you'd make fools of yourselves!'

This was too much for Valentina. 'Just shut up!' she snapped at Rubellina.

'Crys or Jessica would get the part for sure, everyone knows it! They're only refusing to audition so that they can help me get the part. So yah-boo-sucks to you, Rubellina Horrid-Fellow!' She tossed her red hair.

Her friends pulled her away before she could give any more away.

But Rubellina had already started thinking.

CHAPTER THREE
Secret Post

When Jessica went to her locker after lunch the next day, she was surprised to see a envelope stuffed through the locker door-handle. Letters from her family back home normally arrived at breakfast-time, but there had been nothing with her Raspberry Flancakes that morning.

Then she saw the words written on the envelope.

TOP SECRET

Her hands trembled a little as she opened the letter. She let out a little cry of surprise when she saw that a piece of official Palace Theatre golden paper was inside, with its pink-and-gold crest at the top of the page.

Dear Jessica, (said the letter)

I could not help noticing you in your class, and saw that your name was not on the audition list. The part of the Lonely Serving Maid calls for a medium-height, brown-haired Rock Dweller girl, just like you, and nobody else will do. If you come to the auditions, I promise that you will win the part.

Yours,
Aurora Rosmarino

P.S. – Do not tell anyone about this letter, or the Ballet Master will tell me off for interfering.

'Sinbad, look!' Jessica held the letter out for her donkey to read.

Sinbad's eyes grew wide. 'Wow,

Jess, this is amazing! You've as good as got the part!'

'Sinbad, I don't want the part!' said Jessica. 'It's Valentina who needs the part, not me.'

Sinbad remembered it all now. 'But Aurora Rosmarino says they need someone who looks just like you. Valentina doesn't look like you. She looks like a City Dweller.'

'Then we'll just have to make her look like a Rock Dweller before the audition,' said Jessica firmly. 'But this is Top Secret, so we mustn't say a word about this to anyone, Sinbad – not even Valentina herself.'

'Great,' said Sinbad happily. 'I love secrets.'

After tea that afternoon, Jessica and her friends started to help Valentina dress for her audition. Mistress Babette, who adored Valentina, had given special permission for the girls to raid the Costume cupboard.

Jessica and Sinbad quickly found a long brown wig and a raggedy grey old pinafore that looked just like the kind of thing Jessica's Rock-Dwelling sisters always wore.

'Try these, Val,' said Jessica, plonking the wig on Valentina's head. It looked dreadful, and Valentina pulled a face.

'No thanks,' she said. 'I like my own hair better.'

'You're terribly pale, Val.' Laura-Bella

suddenly appeared from the make-up studio with a cake of brown make-up. 'Let me give you a tan.'

'No!' shrieked Jessica, as Laura-Bella started sponging brown make-up on to Valentina's face. If Valentina went nut-brown, like a Valley Dweller, she'd never get the part. 'No make-up!'

'She does need make-up,' said Crys, 'but not to make her tanned. To make her more pale.'

Fighting off Laura-Bella, Crys began to try to brush Valentina's cheeks with a silvery white powder.

'But that will clash with her outfit,'

said Ursula, pushing through, clutching a chiffon scarf in a shade of green that would make Valentina look seasick. 'Try this on, Val!'

Valentina stared at her reflection in the mirror, and let out a shriek. Olympia squawked in sympathy.

'A brown wig, muddy cheeks, a silver nose and a green scarf!' She stood up and ran for the door. 'Some friends! Are you all trying to make me look as bad as possible?'

The door slammed behind her.

'Honestly, you three!' Jessica was angry that the others had all foolishly ruined her plan to make Valentina look the part. 'You've wrecked everything. What were you doing to poor Val?'

'Us?' said Crys. 'What about you? That wig made her look a fright! Anyone would think you didn't want her to get the part after all!'

'Please don't argue,' begged Ursula.

'You were as bad, Ursula,' snapped Laura-Bella. 'Why did you try to make her wear that awful green thing?'

'So that she would look like a Forest Dweller!' Ursula burst out, then clapped a hand over her mouth.

'Oh, no,' whispered her bear, Dorothea. 'You've done it now.'

Jessica stared at Ursula. 'Why were you trying to make Valentina look like a Forest Dweller?'

'No reason,' said Ursula, blushing as

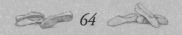

red as a raspberry.

'Then you're very silly!' Sinbad yelled, clattering about on his hoofs. 'She was meant to look like a Rock Dweller, and you ruined everything!'

Jessica sighed, and pulled the Top Secret letter from her pocket . . . just as Crys, Laura-Bella and Ursula all did exactly the same.

'Aurora Rosmarino wrote to tell me the part of the Lonely Serving Maid had to go to a girl looking like a Lake

Dweller,' said Crys, staring at the golden paper in her hand.

'What? Aurora Rosmarino told me it had to be a Valley Dweller,' said Laura-Bella.

Ursula waved her gold letter. 'And here it says that the part is for a

Forest Dweller!'

'We have to go and find Aurora Rosmarino at once,' said Jessica, already hurrying for the door, 'and find out what's going on.'

It was a very out-of-breath and messy Valentina who hurried up to the Great Hall, late for her audition. She had managed to wash off most of the brown tan make-up, and tried to tidy up the mess the brown wig had made of her long, shiny hair. Still, though, she felt rather cross and very, very nervous. Even Olympia's soothing caw-caw noises beside her ear did not make her feel much better.

There was a bored-looking man from the Palace Theatre Company outside the Hall. His pet monkey was holding a clipboard.

'Name?' demanded the monkey

bossily as Valentina dashed up.

'Valentina de la Frou,' she gasped. 'Am I too late to audition?'

'No,' said the monkey, ticking off her name with a quill pen. 'But you'll have to wait. Somebody's in there at the moment.'

Valentina started to do warm-up stretches, using one of the chairs outside the Hall for balance. She took deep breaths to calm her nerves, wishing that her friends were with her

for a final practice and for some encouraging words. Why had they seemed to try so hard to make her look terrible for her audition? It seemed as if they had not wanted her to get the part after all.

Valentina's mood was not improved when the door to the Great Hall suddenly opened, and Rubellina Goodfellow came out of her audition.

'Oh, hello, Val!' she said.

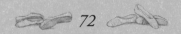

Valentina ignored her. She was soothing Olympia, who was terribly frightened of Rubellina's bully of an eagle, Niccolo.

'My audition went terribly well!' Rubellina did a little pirouette. 'Mind you, I don't think I've got the slightest chance of getting the part.'

'That makes a change,' muttered Valentina. 'You normally think you're the best thing since Toffee Apple Torte.'

Rubellina's blue eyes were wide.

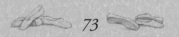

'But I suppose now that Crys has auditioned, none of us stand a chance.'

'What are you talking about?' said Valentina. 'Crys didn't audition.'

'Yes, she did. She was coming out of the Hall as I was going in. Your other friends, too. Jessica, Laura-Bella and that drippy little Ursula. Aurora Rosmarino was being terribly nice to them all.' Rubellina had a triumphant smile on her face. 'I'd be really upset if I were you. Obviously your friends wanted the part more than they wanted to help you stay at school.'

'I don't believe you!' Valentina was shaking. She could feel Olympia quivering, too, on her shoulder.

'I'm sure their names are written down.' Rubellina called over to the monkey. 'Is there a Crys Coldwater on your list?'

The monkey looked at his clipboard.

'Oh, yes. I just ticked her name off when she went in with those three others.' He turned his clipboard round so that Valentina could see the names.

Sure enough, there they all were, with a large gold tick beside each name.

Jessica Juniper.

Crys Coldwater.

Laura-Bella Bergamotta.

Ursula of-the-Boughs.

Valentina sat down very suddenly on one of the chairs.

'What a shame,' trilled Rubellina, as her eagle cawed mockingly. 'Looks like you probably won't be around next term, then!'

'Don't let this stop you,' Olympia whispered in Valentina's ear. 'You've worked so hard, Val – go in there and show Aurora Rosmarino that you should get the part.'

'If you don't go in now,' said the bossy monkey, 'I'm afraid you'll miss your chance.'

Valentina stood up and shook out her long, strawberry blonde hair. 'If I'm going to have to leave here,' she said, 'I may as well say I tried.'

She opened the door of the Great Hall and walked in.

CHAPTER FIVE
Valentina's Last Chance

The audition seemed to be over before Valentina even knew it.

Her heart was pounding so hard at first that she was worried that she might not hear the music. But as soon as the piano started up, and she began to dance for Aurora Rosmarino, everything was as smooth as clockwork.

She remembered every single one of the steps Crys had put together, and was lighter on her feet than ever before. She knew it would be her last chance to dance like this in the Great Hall. Next term it would all be boiled-egg manners and napkin-folding at Madame Malvolio's. When the music came to an end, she had tears in her eyes.

To her surprise, so did Aurora Rosmarino.

'Thank you, Valentina,' said the prima ballerina in her low voice. 'That was a wonderful audition.'

'Just not as wonderful as Crys or Jessica's,' Valentina muttered to herself, knowing that she was about to start crying.

Olympia flew up as Valentina came out of the Great Hall, and wiped away her tears with the tip of her wing.

'Don't cry, Val,' Olympia whispered. 'You'll be the best boiled-egg eater and napkin-folder in the whole Kingdom!'

Heads down, they went up to the dormitory. Valentina pulled her pink-and-gold quilt up over her head, and went to sleep, wishing that she could just vanish.

She woke up, startled, to find herself

being nudged in the ribs by something.

It was Sinbad's nose.

'Valentina, Valentina, wake up!' the donkey was saying.

'Go away,' Valentina grunted.

'But Val, there's great news!' This was Jessica's voice.

Valentina sat up in bed. Her friends were beaming down at her. She glared back. 'Go away.'

'A notice has just gone up, Val,' said Laura-Bella. 'You got the part!'

Valentina's mouth fell open. 'What did you just say?'

'You got the part!' repeated Laura-Bella. 'There's a notice signed by Aurora Rosmarino on the notice board.'

'Really signed by Aurora Rosmarino,' Sinbad added, leaning in to whisper to Valentina and Olympia. 'I always suspected there was something fishy about those Top Secret letters, you know.'

Now Valentina was more confused

than ever. 'Top Secret letters? I don't understand a word any of you are saying!'

Jessica sat down on the bed. 'Somebody played a nasty trick on us all. Each of us was sent a pretend letter saying that the part would only go to someone who looked like us.'

'So that's why you all tried to put me in wigs and strange make-up!' said Valentina.

'But it didn't work!' said Crys.

'And then we all worked out we had the same letter . . .'

'. . . so we went to speak to Aurora Rosmarino to find out what was going on . . .' continued Laura-Bella.

'. . . and she told us she'd never written any such letters . . .' said Ursula.

'. . . so I was right all along,' finished Sinbad, with a toss of his ears.

'But who would have forged the letters?' Valentina gasped.

'There's only one person we know

who could get her hands on official paper like that,' said Jessica. 'The Chancellor's daughter.'

'Rubellina   Goodfellow,'   said

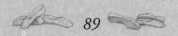

Valentina, falling back against her pillow. 'She wanted to make me think you'd all auditioned so we wouldn't be friends any more.'

'And she wanted to upset you before your audition so you wouldn't get the part,' said Mr Melchior. 'She knew if Crys had been coaching you, you had a much better chance than her.'

Olympia let out a squawk so loud that everybody jumped. 'Val, this is wonderful! You're going to star at the

Palace Theatre, and your mum will be so happy that we can stay at school after all!'

But Valentina shook her head. 'No,

Olympia. It's clear now that Aurora Rosmarino only gave me the part because my friends told her all about me having to go to Madame Malvolio's. Well, she was very kind, but I don't want to have a part I don't deserve.'

All her friends burst out laughing.

'We didn't say a word about Madame Malvolio's!' said Jessica. 'All we did was ask her about the Top Secret letters.'

'You mean I got the part because she really thought I was good enough?'

Valentina gasped.

'Yes, Valentina,' chorused her friends, grinning. 'She really thought you were good enough.'

'In fact,' Jessica added, 'she told us you looked so sad that you made the best Lonely Serving Maid she'd ever seen. So maybe it was a good thing you were upset with us after all!'

Valentina leapt out of bed and started a rowdy dance all around the dormitory, leaping over the beds and spinning her friends about in wild pirouettes.

'What are you weirdos doing?' came a voice from the doorway. It was Rubellina, with her friend Jo-Jo, watching the celebrations with nasty sneers on their faces.

'Haven't you heard?' Sinbad clip-clopped over to them, followed by an adoring Olympia. 'Your plan didn't work.'

Olympia took a deep breath and squared up to Rubellina and her huge,

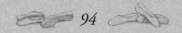

scowling eagle. 'Valentina got the part after all.'

'What?' Rubellina screeched.

'And you can try all you like,' continued Sinbad, heading back with Olympia to join in the dance, 'but you won't stop them all being friends.'

'I don't know what you're talking about, you mangy old donkey,' said Rubellina, as she and Jo-Jo hurried away. 'We've got to get rid of those left-over sheets of official Palace Theatre paper in my locker,' she hissed at Jo-Jo.

'And we'd better cross out the girls' names we wrote on that monkey's clipboard!' said Jo-Jo, far too loudly. 'We should have disguised our handwriting –'

'Jo-Jo, be quiet!' shrieked Rubellina.

Back in the dormitory, the girls all sat down to write a letter to Valentina's mother, telling her the good news. Off Olympia flew to deliver it.

The reply came back just as they were all getting into bed later that evening.

Darling Valentina,

What a clever girl you are! We can't possibly waste a talent like yours at silly old Madame Malvolio's Academy for Better-Brought-Up Young Ladies. You must stay at Ballet School. I can't wait to tell all your aunts and uncles that we're to have a prima ballerina in the family! Now, I must dash, Val – I have to start picking out a new outfit to wear for your opening night.

Love, Mummy

'There's a P.S.,' said Valentina, as her friends crowded around to congratulate her. '"Let's have a celebration at the Grand Tea-Rooms tomorrow. Bring all your friends, dear, but this time please feed that donkey beforehand.'"

And this time, it was the best tea any of them had ever eaten.

THE END

OLYMPIA THE EAGLE'S GUIDE TO
Silverberg

Where to stay

Cheap – Budge Street B&B: a small family-run bed-and-breakfast, with many good points. Unfortunately the good points are not the beds, which are hard and lumpy, nor the breakfasts, which are cold and unappetising.

Service is rude, snappy and sometimes downright nasty. But the views are lovely, and rooms are just a penny a night.

Middling – The Eagle's Wingspan: a cosy inn with an excellent restaurant. Rooms are small but comfortable, with roaring fires and handmade eiderdowns, and cost 1 mark a night.

Expensive – The Silverberg Grand

Hotel: the poshest hotel in town, and Valentina's mother's favourite place in the whole Kingdom. You can choose your room to be painted in whatever colour you like best, and a butler will come and run you a hot bubble bath at any time of the day or night. However, you will need two letters of recommendation and an interview with the hotel manager before you are allowed to stay. The cost of enjoying such luxury is 10 marks a night, but

meeting a friend in the hotel's stunning Ice Bar for a warm glass of Raisin Wine is much cheaper (and one of Madame de la Frou's much-loved hobbies).

What to do

Museums – Why not visit the Museum of Frosty Mountain History and Folklore? Saturdays are the best time to go, when actors in original costumes re-

create the famous Battle of Rushing River from three hundred years ago, when the Lake Dwellers bitterly fought the Forest Dwellers after a quarrel about a quantity of fish. Bring a friend and take sides!

Sights – No visit to Silverberg is complete without a tour of the Royal Palace and the Palace Theatre, which are open to the public every morning. If you are lucky and visit the city out of

term-time, you can also visit the famous Royal Ballet School. Tours are led by teachers at the school, so try to ask for Mistress Camomile or Mistress Babette, and not Master Silas (who will test you on everything) or Master Jacques (who will mime and not say a word).

Shopping – For food and drinks, including the city's famous Cinnamon Twists, go to the market and spend a

morning wandering around over fifty different stalls. For clothes, try Dante's Department Store in Sugarplum Square, where a brand new dress can be made for you by the city's finest tailors in less than an hour. For toys, games and gifts, go to Madame Du Vetiver's Emporium of Treats. This tiny shop, tucked down a small alleyway near Theatre Street, sells every toy you have ever heard of, and many more you haven't.

Where to eat

Breakfast – Start the day with hot buttered Flumpets at Marco's Coffeehouse on Budge Street, but be warned – you will have to queue, and if Marco is in a bad mood, he simply won't make any Flumpets.

Lunch – Ask your hotel to make you some tasty Crumblecheese sandwiches

and eat them on a bench in Sugarplum Square.

Tea – Treat yourself to high tea at the Grand Café and Tea-Rooms. Enjoy a plate of Scoffins with Snowberry Jam, or the famous Toffee Apple Torte.

Supper – Dress up in your best clothes and eat the finest food in the Kingdom at Pierrot's Bistro on Palace Hill. Many of the Kingdom's most famous

Ballerinas have eaten here, so take your autograph book, as you're sure to spot a celebrity or two!

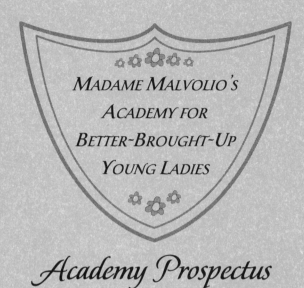

MADAME MALVOLIO'S ACADEMY FOR BETTER-BROUGHT-UP YOUNG LADIES

Academy Prospectus

About the Academy

Located in Snobb House, one of Silverberg's finest mansions, the Academy has been educating better-brought-up young ladies for the last fifty years. It is extremely exclusive, with only twenty pupils. This is excellent for the girls, and even better for their parents, who can lord it over friends whose daughters did not get a place.

About Madame Malvolio

Cordelia Malvolio is one of the most famous women in Silverberg. As a young heiress, her beauty and elegance were legendary, and she was often featured in the gossip columns of the *Silverberg Bugle* and the *Frosty Gazette*. Men came from all over the Kingdom to propose to her, but none was good enough. Instead, Cordelia devoted her life to passing on the secrets of her own beauty and elegance to the lucky young girls who attend her Academy.

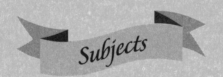

Subjects

(all pupils must study three basic subjects and two advanced ones)

1 **How to eat a boiled egg with charm and grace without soldiers.** (BASIC)

1a How to eat a boiled egg with charm and grace with soldiers. (ADVANCED)

2 How to write a thank-you note for a Christmas present from your favourite uncle. (BASIC)

2a How to write a thank-you note for a Christmas present from your least favourite uncle. (ADVANCED)

3 How to fold a napkin into the shape of a peacock. (BASIC)

3a How to fold a napkin into the shape of a flock of peacocks. (ADVANCED)

④ **How to hire servants.** (BASIC)

④ₐ **How to fire servants.** (ADVANCED)

⑤ **How to plait your hair in eighty-three styles.** (BASIC)

⑤ₐ **How to paint your fingernails in eighty-three colours.** (ADVANCED)

⑥ **How to accept a proposal of marriage.** (BASIC)

⑥ₐ **How to refuse a proposal of marriage.** (ADVANCED)

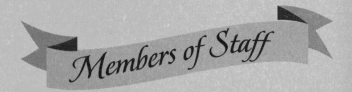

Monsieur DuFour – head of Boiled Egg Studies. Monsieur DuFour has spent many years travelling the Kingdom, making notes on regional egg-eating habits. His textbook Boiled Eggs I Have Known is still the most important work on the subject.

Mistress Kindly – head of the Thank-you Note department. Mistress Kindly would like to thank you for taking the time to read this prospectus. Your interest is most flattering, and she is extremely grateful for your time and effort. She very much looks forward to meeting you in the future.

Mistress Manning – head of Napkin Studies. Mistress Manning won Gold in the Kingdom of the Frosty Mountain's first-ever table-setting Olympics, and still holds the record for the fastest napkin-fold ever, folding one hundred and fifty peacock-shaped napkins in just half an hour.

Madame Bloomingdale – Deputy Head of the Academy, and Head of Servant Management. Madame Bloomingdale has hired and fired servants for almost seventy years. Her strict, no-nonsense approach to firing in particular (voted Most Unpopular Employer in Silverberg for nineteen years running) has won her many admirers, though not among the servant community.

Master Pompadour – head of Hairstyling and Manicures. Master Pompadour is best-known for his creation of Silverberg's must-have hairdo, the Silverberg Sweep. He plans on launching his own range of nail polishes, but is struggling to come up with eighty-three different colours.

Madame Malvolio – Headmistress and Head of Marriage Proposal Studies. See above for details.

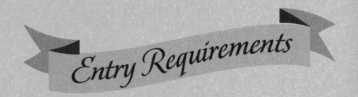

Entry Requirements

Money (plenty of it, please) and a burning desire for bettering yourself. Please apply in writing to: Madame Malvolio, Madame Malvolio's Academy for Better-Brought-Up Young Ladies, Snobb House, Sugarplum Square, Silverberg.

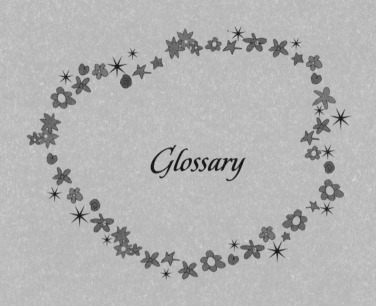

Glossary

Cinnamon Twists: *Long, thin doughnuts that are twisted into a double knot before being freshly fried and then sprinkled with cinnamon sugar. A speciality of Silverberg. Donkeys love them.*

Crocodils and Daffodaisies: Crocodils are yellow or purple wild flowers that grow in spring all over the Kingdom. In fact, wild flowers is a good description – like the crocodiles they sound like, the flowers will give you a little nip on the hand if you try to pick them before they are ready. Daffodaisies are less dangerous. They are tall white-and-yellow daisies the size of daffodils, and perfect for making into long daffodaisy chains.

Frosting-Stones: Precious stones mined from the Frosty Mountains themselves. They come in several colours – red, green, blue and a deep amber – but the most prized of all are the colourless stones, more beautiful even than our own diamonds. The stones come out of the mountain just as they are, with no need for cutting or polishing. Finding a particularly large Frosting-Stone could make your fortune, but mining them is dangerous and difficult work.

Hot Buttered Flumpets: These are a little bit like the crumpets you eat for tea, but they taste softer and slightly sweeter, and they are shaped like fingers. They are always served piping hot, with melted butter oozing through the holes.

Ice Buns: Made for special occasions in the Lakes, these buns look plain on the outside but are filled with creamy pink-and-white ice cream on the inside. Be careful when you bite in!

Iced White Chocolate Drops: An expensive treat that only the very rich can afford. These chocolate drops are found by divers inside seashells at the very bottom of the northern Lake. They stay ice-cold right up until they are popped into your mouth, where they slowly melt.

Icicle Bicycles: Quite simply, bicycles carved from blocks of ice. They are the best way to travel from one side of the

frozen Lake to the other, as the icy wheels speed you across without any danger of skidding or slipping. But be warned, and pack a cushion – or the icy seat will leave your bottom extremely cold.

Lemon Fizzicles: Lemon-flavoured chewy sweets that fizz with tiny bubbles when you suck them.

Raspberry Flancakes: Flancakes are yeasty, flaky pancakes that rise up to five

or ten centimetres thick when you cook them in a special Flancake pan. Their outside is brown and rich with butter, their inside light and airy. Flancakes can be made in any flavour, but raspberry is the most popular. Donkeys love them, too.

Scoffins: Halfway between a scone and a muffin. They are best served fresh from the oven, split in two, and spread with Snowberry Jam.

Snowberries: Round, plump, juicy berries that grow in hedgerows all over the Kingdom throughout the winter. The snowberries from the south and the west are very dark pink, while the ones that grow in the east and the north are red in colour. Snowberries are always eaten cooked – in jams, Flancakes, waffles or muffins – where they taste sweet but tart at the same time. Don't make the mistake of eating one straight from the hedgerow, however tasty it looks. Uncooked

Snowberries are delicious, but they pop open in your mouth and fill it with a juice so sticky that your teeth are instantly glued together. This can take a whole morning to wear off.

SpringSprung Day: The official first day of spring, and a big day for the inhabitants of the Kingdom after a long, cold winter. SpringSprung Day is marked with a big festival in Silverberg, but the Valley Dwellers throw parties in

their own homes for those who would rather not travel the long way to the City. For many, the highlight of the festivities is the SpringSprung Pudding (see below), though many delicious delicacies are served, including lemon-and-orangeade.

SpringSprung Pudding: A sponge pudding, filled with plump currants and chewy dried Snowberries, this is steamed in a huge pudding basin and served in thick slices, sprinkled with sugar, on

SpringSprung Day. One pudding will normally feed ten hungry people. Sinbad can eat a whole pudding all by himself, with room for afters.

Toffee Apple Torte: The speciality of the Grand Café and Tea-Rooms in Silverberg. This tart is made with delicate slices of the fruits that grow in the toffee-apple orchards in the deep south of the Valley, then served warm with toffee-butter sauce.

Who's Who in the Kingdom of the Frosty Mountains

The girls and their pets

Jessica Juniper – *Ballerina from the western Rocks*

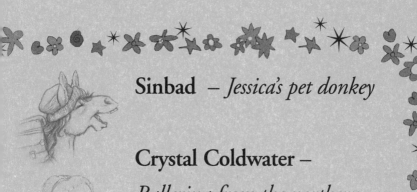

Sinbad – *Jessica's pet donkey*

Crystal Coldwater – *Ballerina from the northern Lake*

Pollux – *Crystal's pet white fox*

Laura-Bella Bergamotta – *Ballerina from the southern Valley*

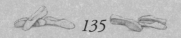

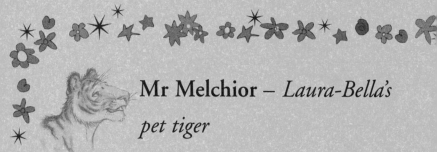

Mr Melchior – *Laura-Bella's pet tiger*

Ursula of the Boughs – *Ballerina from the eastern Forest*

Dorothea – *Ursula's pet bear*

Valentina de la Frou – *Ballerina from the City*

 Olympia – *Valentina's pet eagle*

Some other Ballerinas

Rubellina Goodfellow – *Ballerina from the City, and the Chancellor's daughter*

Jo-Jo Marshall – *Another Ballerina from the City, and Rubellina's best friend*

The Teachers

Mistress Odette – *the Headmistress*

Mistress Camomile – *a Ballet teacher*

Master Lysander – *another Ballet teacher, also known as Mustard Stockings*

Master Silas – *the History of Ballet teacher*

Mistress Hawthorne – *the Gym teacher*

Mistress Babette – *the Costume, Hair and Make-up teacher*

Master Jacques – *the Mime teacher*

The Royal Party

King Caspar – *the King*

Queen Mab – *the Queen*

Chancellor Godwin Goodfellow – *the Kingdom's Chancellor*

Don't miss the first book in the series

Jessica Juniper

It's Jessica's first day at Ballet School
and she wants to make a good
impression. So when the teachers think
she has played a practical joke on the
High Minister's daughter, Jessica and
Sinbad the donkey have to try extra hard.
But things keep going wrong.
Can Jessica prove her innocence?

**Twinkle your toes with the Ballerinas
and their talking pets!**

KINGDOM OF THE
FROSTY MOUNTAINS

Jessica Juniper

by
Emerald
Everhart

Inside the perfume bottle
a magical kingdom is waiting for you . . .

Don't miss the second book in the series

The Ballerinas-in-Training are excited – they have to write about their favourite ballerina, Eva Snowdrop. So why is Crys so upset? Even her fox, Pollux, can't soothe her. Can the girls find out? And how will Icicle Bicycles help?

Twinkle your toes with the Ballerinas and their talking pets!

KINGDOM OF THE FROSTY MOUNTAINS

Crystal Coldwater

by
Emerald
Everhart

Inside the perfume bottle
a magical kingdom is waiting for you . . .

Don't miss the third book in the series

It's SpringSprung time and everyone in
Silverberg is preparing for the Festival.
But Laura-Bella and Mr Melchior the
tiger aren't in the mood to celebrate.
They need to save their family farm.
Their friends want to help, but it means
disobeying the Ballet School rules . . .

**Twinkle your toes with the Ballerinas
and their talking pets!**

KINGDOM OF THE FROSTY MOUNTAINS

Laura-Bella

by Emerald Everhart

Inside the perfume bottle
a magical kingdom is waiting for you . . .

Don't miss the fifth book in the series

Ursula of the Boughs

Ursula wants her father to come
and watch the Ballerinas'
end-of-year concert. But he is
so busy, he doesn't have time.
When the friends see how sad
Ursula and Dorothea her bear are,
they come up with a plan . . .

**Twinkle your toes with the Ballerinas
and their talking pets!**

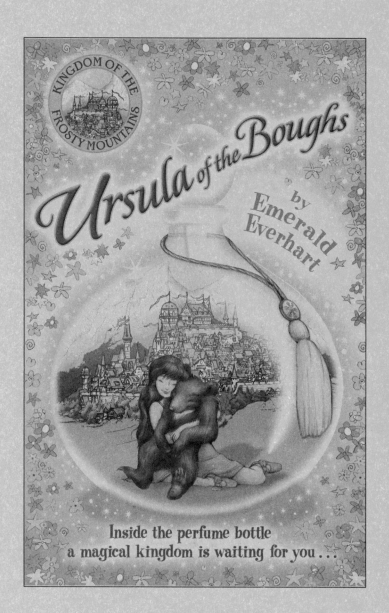

KINGDOM OF THE
FROSTY MOUNTAINS

Ursula of the *Boughs*

by
Emerald
Everhart

Inside the perfume bottle
a magical kingdom is waiting for you . . .

EGMONT PRESS: ETHICAL PUBLISHING

Egmont Press is about turning writers into successful authors and children into passionate readers – producing books that enrich and entertain. As a responsible children's publisher, we go even further, considering the world in which our consumers are growing up.

Safety First
Naturally, all of our books meet legal safety requirements. But we go further than this; every book with play value is tested to the highest standards – if it fails, it's back to the drawing-board.

Made Fairly
We are working to ensure that the workers involved in our supply chain – the people that make our books – are treated with fairness and respect.

Responsible Forestry
We are committed to ensuring all our papers come from environmentally and socially responsible forest sources.

For more information, please visit our website at
www.egmont.co.uk/ethicalpublishing